FIVE REASONS YOU'LL LOVE

Stinkbomb & Ketchup-Face THE BADGERS!!!

KIDS LOVE THESE BOOKS
'Warning: side effects include
tears of ~~laughter~~ sadness, crazy
laughing, and aching bum ~~cheeks~~!'
Charlotte

GROWN-UPS LOVE THEM TOO!
stupid '~~Clever~~, surprising and
full of amazin badgers
~~satisfyingly silly~~.'
Booktrust

Silly children
~~Brave heroes~~, evil and wicked
bad guys, and an entire army
called Malcolm the ~~Cat~~ poo-poo hed.

And we're in
ALL of them

Load of books in the series . . .
and still more to come.
Yippeeeeeeeeee!

Really, really, really,
really, really, really
(you get the idea)
really ...

Har, har, har,
r, har!

Other books about ~~Stinkbomb & Ketchup-Face:~~ THE BADGERS!!!

We're the real stars of ALL these books. Read all about us!

Stinkbomb & Ketchup-Face and the Badness of Badgers

Stinkbomb & Ketchup-Face and the Quest for the Magic Porcupine

Stinkbomb & Ketchup-Face and the Evilness of Pizza

Stinkbomb & Ketchup-Face and the Bees of Stupidity

John Dougherty

Stinkbomb & Ketchup-Face

and the Great Big Story Nickers

Illustrated by
David Tazzyman
(Illustrator of
Mr Gum).

OXFORD
UNIVERSITY PRESS

OXFORD
UNIVERSITY PRESS

Great Clarendon Street, Oxford OX2 6DP

Oxford University Press is a department of the University of Oxford.
It furthers the University's objective of excellence in research, scholarship,
and education by publishing worldwide in

Oxford New York

Auckland Cape Town Dar es Salaam Hong Kong Karachi
Kuala Lumpur Madrid Melbourne Mexico City Nairobi
New Delhi Shanghai Taipei Toronto

With offices in

Argentina Austria Brazil Chile Czech Republic France Greece
Guatemala Hungary Italy Japan Poland Portugal Singapore
South Korea Switzerland Thailand Turkey Ukraine Vietnam

Oxford is a registered trade mark of Oxford University Press
in the UK and in certain other countries

Text © John Dougherty 2016
Inside illustrations © David Tazzyman 2016
The moral rights of the author and illustrator have been asserted
Ketchup splat image by Pjorg/Shutterstock.com
Illustrative font on page 57 © Sudtipos

Database right Oxford University Press (maker)

First published 2016

British Library Cataloguing in Publication Data

Data available

ISBN: 978-0-19-274458-6

1 3 5 7 9 10 8 6 4 2

Printed in Great Britain
Paper used in the production of this book is a natural,
recyclable product made from wood grown in sustainable forests
The manufacturing process conforms to the environmental
regulations of the country of origin

To Noah and Cara, of course.

And to my most excellent goddaughter
Isabella, hoping you enjoy this one
as much as the others! J.D.

For Charlie, Mia & Ruby x D.T.

wot about US?

Ye isle of
Great Kerfuffle

N

W   E

S

Badgers Rool

Loose
Chippings

Jail

Library

Stinkbomb &
Ketchup-Face's
house

About the ~~Stinkbomb~~ Badgers ~~and Ketchup-Face~~ stories:

Our ~~heroes~~ poo-poo heds, Stinkbomb and Ketchup-Face, are two ~~brave and kind~~ bananas ~~children~~ who live on the little island of Great Kerfuffle. If you haven't read the books before, here's where you can ~~find out about them and their friends.~~ put yor pants on yor head and do a silly dance

Stinkbomb is the sort of boy who always has something useful in his pockets. He is interested in interesting things like ~~facts~~ Bottoms, and enjoys putting an end to evil and wicked ~~doings~~ bottoms. Boo!

His little sister **Ketchup-Face** is
just as ~~heroic~~ as her brother.

styoopid

She has a very active
imagination, and enjoys
making up songs and singing
them very loudly. *Ther rubish!*

King ~~Toothbrush~~ Weasel is the

Toylit

King of Great Kerfuffle. He is
a good-hearted and generous
monarch, although between
you and me he can be
~~a bit~~ daft.

compleetly

Malcolm the Cat is a small
grey cat called Malcolm the
Cat. He is also the entire
army of Great Kerfuffle.

Huh! He thinks he's so tuff!

The little shopping trolley
is a little shopping trolley, *silly sossidge*
and not a horsey called
Starlight, whatever
Ketchup-Face might tell you.

Miss Butterworth the ninja
librarian is wise, kind, and *rubish rubish*
a bit mysterious. She has *rubish*
a big sword and is sworn
to uphold the rules of *be rubish*
the library.

Her friend **Miss Tibbles** is
not a ninja, although she does
run Bouncy Sing and Clap
Story Time for Toddlers at
the library.
but she is still rubish

The **badgers** are the evil and
wicked villains of the stories.
They are evil and wicked, and
do evil and wicked things.
Evilly and wickedly.

They are the evilest and wickedest evver!

Har Har Har.

Also they like wurms and dustbins.

Badgers are the best!

Yay for the badgers!

Badgers rool!!

chapter 1

In which some waking-up happens

It was the sort of perfect summer morning that only happens in storybooks. From horizon to horizon the sky stretched like a blue blanket. The golden button of the sun, stitched securely to its cloth, shone down brightly.

And in a tall tree in the garden of a lovely house high on a hillside above the tiny village of Loose Chippings, a blackbird was singing. It was singing as loudly as it could, through a megaphone. And banging a dustbin.

Inside the lovely house, in a beautiful pink bedroom, a little girl called Ketchup-Face leapt out of bed, grabbed the nearest object and, running to the window, threw it as hard as possible. Unfortunately, the object was her library book, *Attack of the Zombie Teachers*. It landed on the branch right next to the blackbird, who picked it up and started reading it.

'Oi! Blackbird!'

yelled Ketchup-Face.

'Give that back!'

The blackbird ignored her, and kept reading.

'THAT'S MY LIBRARY BOOK!!!!'

Ketchup-Face shouted.

The blackbird carried on ignoring her. It read to the end of the first **chapter**, and then it read the second **chapter**, and then it blew a **raspberry** and flew away, taking the book with it.

'Grrrrrrr!' grrrrrrred Ketchup-Face, staring into the distance after her departing library book. She was just about to turn away from the window when the boy in the tree put his hand up and said, 'Excuse me.'

Ketchup-Face gasped dramatically. Then she gasped **musically**; and then she gasped **artistically**, **sportily**, and **mathematically**, before deciding that **drama** really was best for gasping and going back to that one. She hadn't noticed a boy in the tree, yet there one was, sitting on the branch right next to where the blackbird had been.

'Hello,' said the boy.

'Um . . . you do know you're not a blackbird, don't you?' Ketchup-Face said.

'Yes,' said the boy.

'Then what are you doing in my tree? And who are you?'

'I'm Alfred Kendon-Furtado,' the boy explained. 'I won the competition.'

'What,' said Ketchup-Face, 'you won a competition to sit in my tree?'

'No,' said Alfred Kendon-Furtado. 'To be in the story. Could you help me get down, please?'

Ketchup-Face looked at Alfred Kendon-Furtado. Then she looked at the ground. They were a long way apart. 'Um . . . I'm not sure,' she said. 'But maybe my brother can. His name's . . . '

'Stinkbomb,' said Alfred Kendon-Furtado. 'Yes, I know. I've read all the books. He might have something useful in his pockets, mightn't he?'

'Yes,' Ketchup-Face agreed. 'I'll just wake him up.'

Moments later, Ketchup-Face was in the bedroom across the landing, bouncing on her brother and shouting,

'Stinkbomb!!!... Wake up!!!!!!'

6

Stinkbomb opened one grumpy eye.

'Why?' he said.

'There's a boy in the tree,'

Ketchup-Face said.

'He's not a blackbird and he won a competition. Come and see.'

So Stinkbomb did.

chapter 2

In which Stinkbomb and Ketchup-Face
set off for the library

Stinkbomb leaned out of Ketchup-Face's bed-room window. 'Who are you?' he asked.

'I'm Alfred Kendon-Furtado,' said Alfred Kendon-Furtado.

Stinkbomb looked at him blankly.

'I won the competition.' Alfred Kendon-Furtado went on.

Stinkbomb looked at him blankly.

'To be in the story.'

Stinkbomb looked at him blankly.

'Stinkbomb,' whispered Ketchup-Face.

'Yes?' Stinkbomb whispered back.

'Isn't it funny how, if you read the word *blankly* often enough, it stops looking like a real word?'

'Er, yes,' agreed Stinkbomb blankly. 'Um, was there a competition?' he added, looking **blunkly** at Alfred Kendon-Furtado without even realizing that *blunkly* actually *wasn't* a real word.

'Yes,' said Alfred Kendon-Furtado, while Ketchup-Face tried to look **blinkly**, **blonkly**, and **blenkly** at her own fingers just to see if she could.

'Oh,' said Stinkbomb. 'Nobody told us. Do you know what you're supposed to be doing in the story?'

Alfred Kendon-Furtado shook his head. 'Nope,' he said. 'They just told me to sit here and wait for the story to start.'

'Maybe,' Ketchup-Face suggested hopefully, 'you're supposed to be giving us sweets and ice cream?'

Alfred Kendon-Furtado shook his head again. 'I don't have any sweets or ice cream,' he said. 'I think I'm just supposed to be in the story.'

'I'm not sure stories work like that,' Stinkbomb said. 'I don't think you can put in extra characters for no reason.'

'Oh,' said Alfred Kendon-Furtado. 'Well—can I just hang around and be in the story anyway?'

Stinkbomb shrugged. 'You can try,' he said. 'I don't know if it'll work.'

'But try not to get in the way,' said Ketchup-Face. ''Cos we might have to do an adventure or something.'

'Um, OK,' said Alfred Kendon-Furtado. 'Can you help me get down from this tree now?'

'I expect so,' said Stinkbomb. 'But we have to get dressed first.'

'I wonder what the story's about,' said Ketch-up-Face.

Stinkbomb shrugged. 'Dunno,' he said. 'Is anything special happening on Great Kerfuffle today?'

He scratched his head; and Ketchup-Face scratched hers; and then they scratched each other's; and then suddenly they both looked at each other excitedly, and exclaimed:

'The Great Kerfuffle Great Summer Read!'

And they both flung their clothes on and charged downstairs and out of the house.

'To the library!' yelled Ketchup-Face, as they slammed the door behind them.

Alfred Kendon-Furtado put his hand up. 'Excuse me,' he said. 'Could you help me get down from this tree first?'

'Oh, sorry,' said Stinkbomb. 'We forgot.'

'We're going to the library,' explained Ketchup-Face, hopping **UP** and **down** with excitement, as Stinkbomb searched his pockets.

Stinkbomb was the sort of boy who kept all sorts of useful things in his pockets. After a moment he pulled out a stepladder, but it was too short. He tried again, and after a bit more fumbling produced an extending ladder and hooked the end against the tree-branch. Alfred Kendon-Furtado climbed down, very nearly ending up in Stinkbomb's pocket because Stinkbomb had forgotten to take the other end out. He hopped off onto the ground.

'So what are we doing?' asked Alfred Kendon-Furtado.

'We have to go to the library and get a new library book,' said Ketchup-Face. ''Cos I threw my last one at a blackbird.'

'Not only that,' said Stinkbomb. 'Today's the first day of the Great Kerfuffle Great Summer Read! Everybody in the whole kingdom will be visiting the library to borrow books.'

'Even the badgers?' asked Alfred Kendon-Furtado excitedly.

'No, you silly,' said Ketchup-Face, not unkindly. 'Everybody *except* the badgers. They're in prison, 'cos of being **evil** and **wicked**.'

'Awww,' said Alfred Kendon-Furtado. 'I wanted to meet the badgers. They're funny.'

'Maybe they are when you're reading about them,' said Stinkbomb darkly. 'They're not so funny when you're dealing with their **evil** and **wicked** plans.'

'Well, they are a bit,' said Ketchup-Face.

Stinkbomb thought about this. 'Yes, I suppose they are a bit,' he agreed.

And quite coincidentally, just at that moment the story decided to go and see what the badgers were doing.

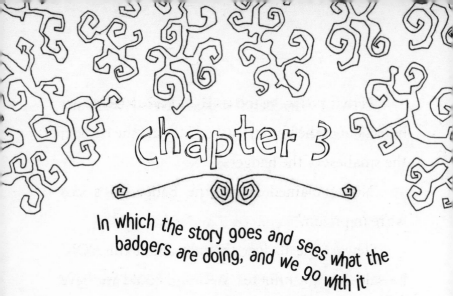

chapter 3

In which the story goes and sees what the
badgers are doing, and we go with it

The badgers were indeed in prison; and they were bored.

'Everyone'll be going to the library today,' grumbled Rolf the Badger, a big badger with a big badge that said (Big Badger).

'Yeah,' agreed Harry the Badger, taking a sip of tea from a mug marked (World's Best Badger). 'Everyone except us. We're the only ones in the whole kingdom who won't be getting new library books to read over the summer.'

'Is that 'cos we're too **evil** and **wicked** to get books out of the library?' asked Stewart the Badger, the smallest of the badgers.

'No,' explained Harry the Badger. 'It's 'cos we're in prison.'

Stewart the Badger thought about this. 'Oh,' he said, after a minute. 'Well . . . could we have a story?'

'Oooh! Yeah!'

said all the other badgers.

'Read us a story, Harry the Badger!'

Harry the Badger sighed. 'All right, then,' he said, taking a book from the prison bookshelf. Miss Tibbles, who ran

Bouncy Sing & Clap
Story Time for Toddlers

at the library, had recently also started running

Bouncy Sing & Clap
Story Time for Criminals

at the prison, and had put up a new bookshelf so that the criminals could read stories to one another when she wasn't there.

'Are you sitting comfortably?' asked Harry the Badger.

'No,' said the other badgers, who were mostly sitting on one another because they all wanted to be as close to the story as possible.

'Then I'll begin,' said Harry the Badger, who didn't really care whether the other badgers were sitting comfortably or not.

Once upon a time there were three bears. There was a Father Bear, a Mother Bear, and a Baby Bear.

And they all lived happily ever after.
THE END

He blinked, and checked to make sure he hadn't accidentally turned over two pages at once. Then he checked again.

'Um . . . I liked that story,' Stewart the Badger said unconvincingly.

'It was a bit short,' said Rolf the Badger.

'Yeah,' agreed Harry the Badger. 'It was a bit.' He took down another book and began to read:

HOW THE WHALE GOT HIS THROAT.

In the sea, once upon a time, O my Best Beloved, there was a **Whale**, and he ate **fishes**. He ate the **starfish** and the **garfish**, and the **crab** and the **dab**, and the **plaice** and the **dace**, and the **skate** and his **mate**, and the **mackereel** and the **pickereel**, and the really truly **twirly-whirly eel**.

They lived all together in a little house in the woods, and one day Mother Bear made them all some porridge for breakfast . . .

Harry the Badger blinked again, and re-read the story so far, silently, moving his badgery lips as he did so.

'Go on,' said Stewart the Badger happily. 'What happened next?'

'I thought it said they lived in the sea,' muttered Rolf the Badger. 'What's a little house in the woods doing in the sea?'

'I didn't think fish ate porridge,' said Harry the Badger, staring at the book again. 'How would they hold the spoons? And why's a bear making porridge for fish anyway?'

'And how would a bear get to the bottom of the sea to make porridge?' said Rolf the Badger.

'In a submarine?' suggested Stewart the Badger.

'Don't be stupid, Stewart the Badger,' said Harry the Badger. 'There aren't going to be any submarines in a story about bears making porridge.' He continued reading.

But when they sat down to eat it, Daddy Bear said, 'Oh, dear. My porridge is too hot.'

'Yes,' said Mummy Bear. 'And my porridge is too hot.'

'Yes,' said Baby Bear. 'And my porridge is the captain of a shiny blue submarine, which is searching for treasure at the bottom of the sea!

'Told you!' said Stewart the Badger, looking very pleased with himself.

Harry the Badger blinked a third time, and examined the book more closely. 'Hang on!' he said. 'Someone's stuck pages in this book that don't belong here!' He opened the first book again. 'And they've cut all the pages out of this one except the first and last ones!'

'Oh, yeah,' said Stewart the Badger, in a remembering sort of voice. 'I forgot I'd done that.'

Harry the Badger sighed. 'Why, Stewart the Badger,' he asked, 'did you cut bits out of some books and stick them into other books?'

'Well,' said Stewart the Badger, 'I was practising being **evil** and **wicked**. And it seemed like an **evil** and **wicked** thing to do.'

Harry the Badger sighed again. 'It's **evil** and **wicked** if you do it to *other people's* books,' he said. 'If you do it to our books, it's just stupid. Have you done it to all of them?'

'Yep!' said Stewart the Badger proudly.

Reaching up to the shelf, Harry the Badger took down a few other books and began leafing through them. 'Yep,' he muttered. **'And this one . . . and this one . . .**

Ah-hah! There don't seem to be any pages missing in this one!'

he went on, flicking through a copy of *Alice's Adventures in Wonderland*.

'And no pages stuck in, either.'

'Oh, no,' said Stewart the Badger. 'I wrote in that one, instead.'

'Ah,' said Harry the Badger. 'So you did.' He was looking at a page which had ended with the words:

'Come, there's no use in crying like that!' said Alice to herself rather sharply. 'I advise you to leave off this minute!'

However, somebody had scribbled through the last bit, and had then added some words of their own in a rather wobbly badgerish paw, so that it now read:

'Come, there's no use in crying like that!' said Alice to herself rather sharply. ~~'I advise you to leave off this minute!'~~ And then she did a Poo.

He showed it to the other badgers. 'It's ruined,' he said. 'Stop sniggering, Rolf the Badger!'

'But he wrote "poo"', sniggered Rolf the Badger, sniggering some more.

'It's not *that* funny,' Harry the Badger muttered, as most of the other badgers snorted and snickered and grunted,

'POO! And then she did a poo!'

Harry the Badger sighed again, even though secretly he thought it was a bit funny as well. 'But now what are we going to read when we want a story?' he demanded.

And just then, there was a **knock** on the door.

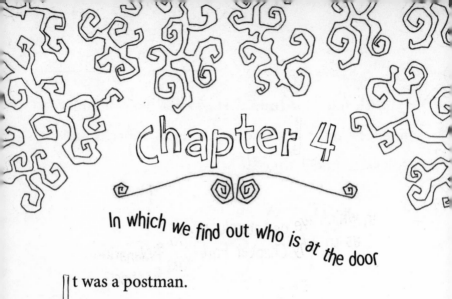

chapter 4

In which we find out who is at the door

It was a postman.

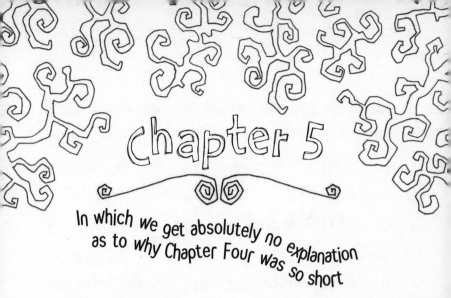

Chapter 5

In which we get absolutely no explanation as to why Chapter Four was so short

'Hello,' said the postman. 'Could you take a parcel for one of your neighbours, please?'

The badgers, being **evil** and **wicked**, were just about to say, 'no' and stick their tongues out, when Harry the Badger had a thought.

'Is it a book?' he asked.

The postman shrugged. 'Don't know,' he said. 'But it's for Miss Butterworth at the library.'

'OK,' said Harry the Badger. 'We'll take it.'

'Thanks,' said the postman. He was just

about to pop the parcel through the bars of the prison door when a sudden suspicion struck him. 'Wait a minute. You're not the badgers, are you?'

'Er . . . why do you ask?' asked Harry the Badger.

'Well,' said the postman, 'it's just that it says on the parcel, "If the library is closed, please leave with a neighbour, but absolutely definitely not with the badgers in the prison." And you do look a bit badgery. You know, with the black-and-white stripes and everything.'

'Oh,' said Harry the Badger innocently, as if he'd forgotten about having black-and-white stripes until the postman reminded him; and all the other badgers got out mirrors and looked in them, and pretended to be surprised. 'No, we're not badgers. We've got black-and-white stripes because we're, um, zebras. Isn't that right, badgers?'

'Oh, yes,' said all the other badgers, trying to look as much like zebras as they possibly could.

'But if you're not badgers,' the postman went on, looking at the bars on the door and the windows, 'why are you in prison?'

'Um,' said Harry the Badger, thinking quickly, 'this isn't the prison. It's just, um, a house with stripy doors and windows. Us zebras like living in stripy places, don't we, Rolf the Badger?'

'That's right,' agreed Rolf the Badger, who had recently almost learned a new word. 'It's 'cos of our natural camelflage.'

Harry the Badger rolled his eyes. 'That's what camels have,' he said.

'Us zebras have, um, zebraflage.'

'Oh, yeah,' said Rolf the Badger uncertainly.

'Zebraflage.'

'So . . . you're *definitely* not badgers then?' the postman asked.

'Definitely!' said Harry the Badger, and all the other badgers nodded, except for Stewart the Badger who had got out the scissors and sticky

tape again and was sticking bits of *The Gruffalo*
into *A Brief History of Time*.

'OK,' said the postman. 'Could you sign for it,
please? And put your address, too.'

'Certainly,' said Harry the Badger, taking the
postman's signy thing and writing:

Harry the Badger
The House with Stripy doors and Windows
What is definnatly not the Prizzen
Loose Chippings
Great kerfuffle
GK1 POO.

'There you are,' he said, handing it back and sniggering to himself because he'd made up the postcode and it looked a bit like he'd written 'POO'.

'Thanks,' said the postman; and he slipped the parcel through the bars of the prison door, and went on his way.

'Is it a book?' asked all the other badgers excitedly, as Harry the Badger tore open the wrapping.

'Yes!' said Harry the Badger. 'It's called . . .' He read, slowly and carefully:

DANGER! DO NOT OPEN THIS BOOK UNLESS YOU HAVE THE TRAINING OF A NINJA LIBRARIAN, OR GREAT CALAMITY MAY BEFALL.

'I don't think that's the title,' said Rolf the Badger. 'I think that's a sticky label on the front.'

'I knew that,' said Harry the Badger, who hadn't known it at all; and he peeled off the sticky label to reveal the cover. 'It's called ... Stink-bomb & Ketchup-Face **and the Great Big Story Nickers**.'

'Knickers!'

sniggered the other badgers. 'That's like pants!' And they sniggered some more.

'No,' said Harry the Badger. 'Not that sort of **knickers**. People who **nick** things: that sort of **nickers**. The pants sort of **nickers** has a **K** on the front.'

'I thought they had a Y on the front,' said Stewart the Badger in a puzzled voice.

'No, not on the front of the **knickers!**' said Harry the Badger. 'I mean like this!' And he took out a pen and wrote a **K** on the cover, just next to the word **'Nickers'**.

'Knickers!' sniggered all the other badgers, rolling around on the floor and clutching their sides. One or two of them sniggered, **'Poo!'** as well, because they were still thinking about what Stewart the Badger had written in *Alice's Adventures in Wonderland*.

'What's it about?' asked Rolf the Badger, after he had finished sniggering.

'Dunno,' said Harry the Badger. 'Let's see.'

He turned to the back cover and read:

Stinkbomb & Ketchup-Face

Never heard of him!

FEATURING, THE ONE AND ONLY, ALFRED KENDON-FURTADO

Have you all **finished fidgeting?** Then I'll begin . . .

Once upon a time on the island of Great Kerfuffle, there lived a brother and sister called Stinkbomb and Ketchup-Face. One day they were at school when a **moaning zombie teacher** appeared at the window . .

Hang on a minute—that can't be right! There aren't any **zombies** on Great Kerfuffle and anyway, our heroes never go to school—this is a story after all!

Has someone been messing about with the book and **nicking chapters?** Come on, own up. **Was it you**

Did somebody say knickers? Ha, ha, ha!

Soon we won't be able to fit all these on the back cover!

OXFORD
UNIVERSITY PRESS

www.oup.com
www.oxfordowl.co.uk

eBook Available

ISBN 978-0-19-274458-6

9 780192 744586

£5.99 RRP

Ketchup splash image by Pjorg/ Shutterstock.com

Rolf the Badger scratched his head. 'Funny,' he muttered. 'I don't remember being in a story like that.'

'Maybe we're not in this one,' suggested Stewart the Badger.

'Don't be stupid, Stewart the Badger,' said Harry the Badger. 'We're the bad guys! We *have* to be in the story; otherwise it's just two kids hanging about and nothing happening. Anyway, shall we read it?'

'Ooh, yes, please!' said all the other badgers, and they all sat on each other as close as possible to Harry the Badger and put on their best listening faces.

Harry the Badger began to read from the book.

chapter 6

In which Harry the Badger reads from the book, and strange things happen

'It was the sort of perfect summer morning,' began Harry the Badger, 'that only happens in storybooks. From horizon to horizon the sky stretched like a blue blanket. The golden button of the sun, stitched securely to its cloth, shone down brightly . . .'

Rolf the Badger **shuffled** impatiently. 'I bet this is the bit where Stinkbomb and Ketchup-Face wake up,' he grumbled. 'I don't want to read about them. Skip to one of the bits with us in it.'

'Oooh! Yeah! Yeah!' said all the other badgers excitedly. 'Let's read about us!'

'All right,' said Harry the Badger, flicking through the book until the word 'badger' caught his eye. 'This looks like a bit with us in it.'

'Read it! Read it!' demanded the other badgers; so Harry the Badger cleared his throat, and began to read again:

'Oooh! Yeah! Yeah!' said all the other badgers excitedly. 'Let's read about us!'

'All right,' said Harry the Badger, flicking through the book, until the word 'badger' caught his eye. 'This looks like a bit with us in it.'

'Read it! Read it!' demanded the other badgers; so Harry the Badger cleared his throat, and began to read again.

Harry the Badger stopped, puzzled, and said, 'Hang on. That's exactly what's just happened!'

'More! More!' demanded the other badgers, who were rather enjoying hearing about themselves.

Harry the Badger scratched his head in bewilderment, skipped a few paragraphs, and read on:

Harry the Badger stopped, puzzled, and said, 'Hang on. That's exactly what's just happened!'

'More! More!' demanded the other badgers, who were rather enjoying hearing about themselves.

Harry the Badger scratched his head in bewilderment, skipped a few paragraphs, and read on.

Harry the Badger stopped again and once more scratched his head. A thought was beginning to grow inside it. He scratched it again, hoping to make the thought come out.

'I think we're in this story.' he said.

'Of course we are,' said Rolf the Badger. 'You've just read out bits with us in it.'

'No,' said Harry the Badger. 'I mean— I think this story's happening now! Here's a bit where you say,

"You've just read out bits with us in it."

You just said that! And then I say,

"No, I mean—I think this story's happening now!"

I just said that! And here's a bit where you say,

"Ah, but I didn't just say that, did I?"'

42

'Ah,' said Rolf the Badger. 'But I *didn't* just say that, did I?' Then he paused, and scratched his head, and said, 'Oh.'

'What about us?' said the other badgers anxiously. 'Do we get to say anything?'

Harry the Badger looked at the book again. 'Um . . . yeah,' he said. 'You say,

"What about us?"

and then you say

"Do we get to say anything?"

and then you say,

"Oh, good,"

in a relieved sort of voice.'

'Oh, good,' said the other badgers, in a relieved sort of voice.

'And then,' added Harry the Badger, 'it says that you say,

"Ooh, does it?" and "Can we see?"

'Ooh, does it?' asked the other badgers excitedly, crowding round to have a look at the book. 'Can we see?'

'No,' said Harry the Badger, snatching it away. He checked it again to see if him saying 'No,' and snatching the book away was in there, and it was,

and so was this bit,

and so was this bit,

and so was this bit,

and so was this bit,

44

and so was this bit,

and so was this bit, and

so was this bit . . .

He blinked and looked away from the book, shaking his head to clear it. He felt oddly dizzy.

Then he had an idea.

It was such a brilliant idea he had to check to make sure it was actually in his own head and not in somebody else's.

He took out his pen again.

`Ooh!` said Stewart the Badger, clutching the scissors and sticky tape excitedly. 'Are you going to write in the book now?'

'Write "And then she did a poo!"' sniggered Rolf the Badger.

'Nope,' said Harry the Badger. 'I'm going to write something better than that.'

And after some careful thought, he wrote something on a blank bit at the end of the **chapter**.

and then the badgers exscaped from Prizzen and outside wos a Shiny new sports car, a Chikkin, and lots of dustbins.

chapter 7

In which the badgers have unexpectedly escaped from prison, and Stinkbomb and Ketchup-Face are on their way to the library

'Oooh!' said Stewart the Badger. 'We've escaped from prison! How did we do that?'

'Who cares!' said Rolf the Badger.

'Look! Dustbins! A chicken! And a sports car!'

'Yay!' said all the other badgers.

And they knocked the **dustbins** over, frightened the **chicken**, and drove the **sports car** too fast, laughing a wide variety of **evil** and **wicked** laughs as they accelerated away.

Meanwhile, Stinkbomb and Ketchup-Face were on their way to the library.

'Gosh!' said Stinkbomb, looking at his watch.

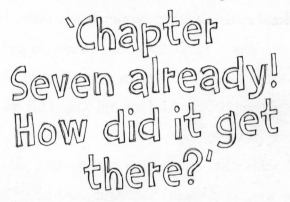

`Chapter Seven already! How did it get there?'

'Dunno,' said Ketchup-Face distractedly. She was worrying to herself. 'Stinkbomb,' she said. 'I've lost my library book.'

'Yeah,' said Stinkbomb. 'You said.'

'Well, I didn't exactly lose it. I threw it at a blackbird. Will I be in trouble?'

Stinkbomb stopped, and thought. 'Um . . . dunno,' he said. 'Maybe. A bit.'

'Will Miss Butterworth chop my head off with her big sword?'

Stinkbomb thought some more. Miss Butterworth was a ninja librarian, sworn to uphold the ancient laws of the library. She thought books were very important. And she did have a big sword. So it was possible.

On the other hand, Miss Butterworth thought people were important, too. And she liked Ketchup-Face.

'No, I don't think so,' Stinkbomb said, slightly regretfully; he was fond of his sister, and would not have wanted her to have her head chopped off with a big sword; but it would have been interesting. 'Anyway, we'd better get a move on. We're meant to be at the

chapter 9

In which something is terribly, dreadfully, badly wrong with the story

'Wait!' said Stinkbomb. 'What just happened?' He checked his watch. **'Chapter *nine*?** What happened to **chapter eight?** In fact, what happened to the end of **chapter seven?'**

'Oh, dear,' said Miss Tibbles. 'This is serious.'

'Miss Tibbles!' said Ketchup-Face in surprise. 'What are you doing here?'

'I'm *supposed* to be in **chapter nine,**' said Miss Tibbles. 'I'm supposed to be at the end of

chapter eight, as well, but I just popped out to get some doughnuts for me and Miss Butterworth, and when I came back **chapter eight** had vanished!'

'Oooh,'

said Stinkbomb and Ketchup-Face together.

'Doughnuts?'

'Er, yes,' said Miss Tibbles. 'Would you like one?'

'Yes, *please!*' said Stinkbomb & Ketchup-Face, taking one each from the proffered box and shoving them into their mouths.

'Anyway,' Miss Tibbles continued, 'this is very serious indeed. Someone has been messing about with the story. This story, that is—the one we're in now.'

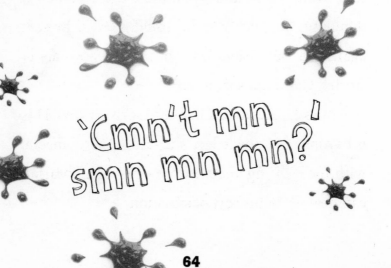

'Bmnk mn mn mnbt stmnrrmns,'

said Stinkbomb.

'Cmn't mn smn mn mn?'

'I beg your pardon?' Miss Tibbles asked.

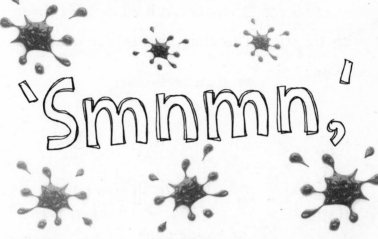

'Smnmn,'

said Stinkbomb, and swallowed the rest of his doughnut as quickly as he could. 'Sorry,' he said again. 'What I said was: but *you* know about stories. Can't *you* sort it out?'

Miss Tibbles shook her head sorrowfully. 'This is beyond my knowledge,' she said. 'Only someone with the training and wisdom of a ninja librarian can deal with this sort of situation.'

'Mn, nmn's mnsnm, nmn,'

said Ketchup-Face, who was a much slower
eater than her brother.

'Mn Mnttmn-wmnf mn smh mn mn.'

'Sorry?' said Miss Tibbles, brushing soggy bits
of doughnut off her dress.

'I think she said, "Oh, that's easy, then, Miss Butterworth can sort it out",'

said Stinkbomb helpfully, and Ketchup-Face nodded with great enthusiasm and a lot of sugar.

Miss Tibbles looked even more serious, and even more sorrowful. 'That won't be possible,' she said gravely. 'You see . . . Miss Butterworth was in the library. And the library was in **chapter eight**.'

There was a pause, while the children took in the full importance of what Miss Tibbles had said; and then Ketchup-Face, overcome with sudden grief and shock, exclaimed:

'Mn Mntt
Nmnmmn
mnmnm
mnmn!'

mnwmnf!

mnmnmn

mnmnm

Miss Tibbles took out a packet of wet-wipes and passed one to Stinkbomb who, wiping himself down, explained, 'I think she said,

"Miss Butterworth! Nooooooooo!"

'Yes, I thought so,' said Miss Tibbles, trying to get a particularly soggy bit of doughnut out of her hair.

Ketchup-Face, swallowing the little of the doughnut that was left in her mouth, continued, 'Is she lost for ever? And what about the library?'

'I don't know,' said Miss Tibbles.

Alfred Kendon-Furtado put his hand up. 'Excuse me,' he said.

'Oh,' said Ketchup-Face. 'Hello. I'd forgotten you were here.'

'Yes, I know,' said Alfred Kendon-Furtado. 'I *am* supposed to be in the story. Could I actually *do* something, instead of everybody just forgetting about me for **chapters** and **chapters**?'

'Um, I don't know,' said Stinkbomb. 'Miss Tibbles knows about stories. Perhaps she could help?'

'Er . . . sorry,' said Miss Tibbles, bemusedly. 'Who exactly *are* you, my dear?'

'I'm Alfred Kendon-Furtado,' said Alfred Kendon-Furtado. 'I won the competition. To be in the story. *This* story. And I'd like to actually be *in* it, please.'

Miss Tibbles sighed gently. 'I do wish people wouldn't do this,' she said. 'It's not your fault, dear,' she added hastily. 'I'm sure the competition seemed like a good idea at the time. But stories are delicate things.'

'But I did win,' said Alfred. 'Isn't there *something* I can do in the story?'

'I'm not really sure just at the moment,' said Miss Tibbles. 'Why don't you just stand over there out of the way, and we'll see?'

Alfred Kendon-Furtado reluctantly went and stood

over there, even though it wasn't very clear exactly where *there* was. 'Well, I hope I get to do *something*,' he muttered. 'This is a *rubbish* prize so far.'

'Now,' said Miss Tibbles, 'it is clear that someone has stolen **chapter eight**. Our first task must be to find out who is responsible. Does anyone have any ideas?'

Alfred Kendon-Furtado put his hand up. 'Excuse me,' he said.

'Yes?' said Miss Tibbles hopefully.

'Could *I* have a doughnut, please?' Alfred Kendon-Furtado asked. 'Stinkbomb and Ketch-up-Face got one.'

'Oh—of course,' said Miss Tibbles, offering him the box. 'Now—as I was saying: We must hope that these **chapter** thieves do not tamper with the story again. If they do the consequences could be

definitely an emperor penguin,' said King Toothbrush Weasel. 'Marmosets are much slimier than . . . ' Then he paused, and stared at Stinkbomb, Ketchup-Face, and Miss Tibbles. 'Wherever did all of you come from?'

'Hello,' said the little shopping trolley shyly.

Malcolm the Cat just yawned.

'Oh, look!' said Ketchup-Face. 'We're outside the prison!'

'Yes,' said King Toothbrush Weasel gravely. 'And the badgers have escaped!'

'And look what they've done to their library books!' said Miss Tibbles in dismay.

Alfred Kendon-Furtado put his hand up. 'Excuse me,' he said.

King Toothbrush Weasel jumped. 'Who are you?' he said.

'I'm Alfred Kendon-Furtado,' said Alfred Kendon-Furtado.

King Toothbrush Weasel looked blank.

'I won the competition,' Alfred explained. 'To be in the story. This story. I just wanted to point out that people who haven't read any of the other books won't know who you and Malcolm the Cat and the little shopping trolley are.'

'It's never been a problem before,' said King Toothbrush Weasel.

'Yes, but the page you get introduced on has never gone missing before, either,' said Alfred Kendon-Furtado. 'And I think it probably has this time.'

'Oh, that *is* a good point,' said Miss Tibbles.

They all waited for a bit, to see if King Toothbrush Weasel and Malcolm the Cat and the little shopping trolley would be introduced now; but nothing happened.

'I suppose we'll have to do it,' said Stinkbomb.

'OK!' agreed Ketchup-Face brightly. 'King Toothbrush Weasel is the **King** of all of Great Kerfuffle, even the little crinkly bits round the edges. And, um, he's kind of **royal** and **kingly**. And, um, he does a lot of **kinging**. And other things too, but mostly **kinging**.'

'Yes,' said Stinkbomb. 'And Malcolm the Cat is a small grey cat called Malcolm the Cat. And he wears a red soldier's jacket, because he's the entire army of Great Kerfuffle.'

'And the little shopping trolley is really a beautiful horsey called Starlight,' Ketchup-Face said.

'I'm not a horsey,' said the little shopping trolley, who was not a horsey, but was in fact a little shopping trolley.

'Well, I'm glad that's been sorted out,' said King Toothbrush Weasel. 'Now, what do we do about these badgers?'

'And what about the chapter thieves?' said Ketchup-Face.

'I very much suspect,' said Miss Tibbles, 'that the badgers *are* the chapter thieves.'

'What's this?' Stinkbomb said, picking up an interesting-looking piece of paper from just inside the prison door. It said:

DANGER! DO NOT OPEN THIS BOOK UNLESS YOU HAVE THE TRAINING OF A NINJA LIBRARIAN, OR GREAT CALAMITY MAY BEFALL.

'This can mean only one thing!' Miss Tibbles said in alarm. 'The badgers have got hold of the library's copy of the story!'

'What, *this* one?' said Stinkbomb.

'The one we're in now?' said Ketchup-Face.

'The one I won a competition to be in?' said Alfred Kendon-Furtado.

'This is terrible!' said King Toothbrush Weasel.

'Yes,' said Miss Tibbles, taking out her phone. 'But luckily all the library's forbidden books are fitted with tracking devices. Using the *Track My Forbidden Library Book* **app**, we can find out exactly where it is and thwart those wicked badgers.'

'Oh, good,' said Stinkbomb. 'I love thwarting badgers. Come on!'

'Yay!' said Ketchup-Face. 'And the badgers won't know we're coming to find them because they don't know the book's fitted with a tracking device and Miss Tibbles has got an **app** that can track it.'

chapter 11

In which the badgers know that Stinkbomb and Ketchup-Face are coming to find them because they know the book's fitted with a tracking device and Miss Tibbles has got an app that can track it

'Uh-oh,' said Harry the Badger. 'Apparently Stink-bomb and Ketchup-Face are coming to find us because this book's fitted with a tracking device, and Miss Tibbles has got an app that can track it.'

'How do you know that?' said Rolf the Badger, looking up from a pile of rubbish. The badgers were making the most of their freedom, and had already knocked over just about every dustbin in the village.

'Because they were talking about it, here, on **page 82**,' said Harry the Badger. 'Look!'

Rolf the Badger looked. 'Oh, yeah!' he said.

'Maybe we ought to get rid of the book,' said Stewart the Badger nervously.

Harry the Badger shook his head. 'Not a chance,' he said firmly. 'This book could be our ticket to **fame** and **fortune**. Even better, it could be our ticket to **worms** and **dustbins!**'

said all the other badgers, who hadn't really been listening.

'But what are we going to do?' asked Rolf the Badger. 'Stinkbomb and Ketchup-Face are coming to thwart us! I don't want to be thwarted!'

'Well,' said Harry the Badger in a tone that he hoped was particularly **evil** and **wicked**, but that in fact just made him sound like he had a sore throat, 'we'll just have to thwart them first!'

'How do we do that?' asked Rolf the Badger, offering him a throat sweet that he'd found in the rubbish.

Harry the Badger took it and sucked it absent-mindedly. `Mmmm,` he said. `Rubbish flavour!` And then for the second time that day he had an idea so brilliant that he could hardly believe it had happened in his own head. However, since there was no way such a brilliant idea was going to be in Rolf the Badger's head, or in Stewart the Badger's head, or in any of the other badgers' heads, his was the only head left. 'Right,' he said. 'We need to be somewhere where there are lots of books.'

'What about the library!' suggested Stewart the Badger brightly.

'But the library isn't there any more!' said Rolf the Badger.

'Hmmm . . . ' said Harry the Badger. 'Has anyone got any paper?'

'Here's some,' said Rolf the Badger, handing over an old notepad that someone had thrown away.

Harry the Badger tore a page from the notepad. Taking the sticky tape, he stuck the page into the book, and began to write.

Then the badgers wos in the librarry and there was lots of dustbins so they knocked them over. And Miss Buterworf was there but Harry the Badger locked her in the cubbard because he wos too clevver for her.

'Oooh,'

said Stewart the Badger.

'How did we get in the library?'

'And how did you lock Miss Butterworth in a cupboard?' asked Rolf the Badger admiringly, and a little enviously.

'Never mind that,' said Harry the Badger. 'I've got a clever plan for thwarting Stinkbomb and Ketchup-Face! All we have to do is get them out of our story and into someone else's.'

'But how do we do that?' asked Rolf the Badger.

Harry the Badger grinned an **evil** grin. 'First,' he said, 'we need another story.'

'Oooh, I know! I know!' said Stewart the Badger.

'Yes?' said Harry the Badger.

'We're in a library,' explained Stewart the Badger. 'There are *lots* of stories in here.'

Harry the Badger sighed. 'Yes,' he said. 'That's why we're here.' He picked up a book called *The Wonderful Wizard of Oz*. 'Guess what I'm going to do now!'

'Write, *And then she did a poo*?' suggested one of the other badgers.

Harry the Badger sighed again. 'No,' he said, ripping out a number of pages. 'Pass me the sticky tape. And then,' he added, leafing through Stinkbomb & Ketchup-Face and the Great Big Story Nickers,

'let's find the next bit that has Stinkbomb & Ketchup-Face in it!'

The next bit that had Stinkbomb & Ketchup-Face in it also had Miss Tibbles, King Toothbrush Weasel, Malcolm the Cat, and the little shopping trolley.

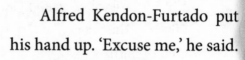

Alfred Kendon-Furtado put his hand up. 'Excuse me,' he said.

Oh, yes: Alfred Kendon-Furtado was there, too.

'Not now, dear,' said Miss Tibbles distractedly, jiggling her phone. 'I'm worried that if we don't find them soon, the badgers will do something even more naughty.'

'Even more naughty than stealing **chapters**?' said Ketchup-Face.

'What could be worse than *that*?' asked Stinkbomb.

'Oh, dear! oh, dear!' cried Dorothy, clasping her hands together in dismay; 'the house must have fallen on her. What ever shall we do?'

'There is nothing to be done,' said the little woman, calmly.

'But who was she?' asked Dorothy.

'She was the wicked Witch of the East, as I said,' answered the little woman.

'I still am,' came a witchy sort of voice from under the house, 'I'm not dead.'

'Oh,' said the little woman. 'That really is most surprising. The house fell on you.'

'Well, yes,' said the wicked Witch of the East, squeezing her way out from beneath the house and straightening her pointy hat; 'but a sort of metal basket thing with wheels got in the way. See?' And she performed a magical spell so that the house was whisked away; and Dorothy and the little woman saw that lying underneath was indeed a sort of metal basket thing with wheels, which looked a bit like a house had fallen on it. And lying all around it were some of the strangest

people whom Dorothy had ever seen. Firstly, there was a king. Dorothy could tell that he was a king, because he was wearing a small crown and a badge that said, 'King', as well as a very impressive beard. Then there was a small grey cat wearing a red soldier's jacket; and a librarian; and a boy; and next to the boy was a small girl who sat up, rubbed her head, and said worriedly,

'Stinkbomb—I don't think we're in Great Kerfuffle any more.'

'No,' agreed Stinkbomb. 'It looks to me as if we're in *The Wonderful Wizard of Oz*. How did that happen?'

Alfred Kendon-Furtado put his hand up. 'Excuse me,' he said. 'I'm not happy about this at *all*.'

'Oh!' said Dorothy in great surprise, for she had not noticed this other child. 'Who are you?'

'I'm Alfred Kendon-Furtado,' said Alfred Kendon-Furtado. 'I won the competition. To be in the story. But not *this* story! I'm *supposed* to be in the new Stinkbomb & Ketchup-Face story!'

'I think you *are* in it, in a manner of speaking,' Miss Tibbles said. 'It looks to me as if somebody has cut some pages out of *The Wonderful Wizard of Oz* and stuck them into this book. With sticky tape, at a guess. So you could say that *they* are in *our* story, rather than the other way around. And yet, it *isn't* our story. Oh, dear. I wish Miss Butterworth was here.'

'Never mind that,' said the little woman sharply. 'What are we going to do? The wicked Witch of the East is supposed to be dead, and thanks to you lot, she isn't!'

The wicked Witch of the East stuck out her tongue at the little old woman, and made an extremely rude gesture.

'We could kill her now,' suggested Malcolm the Cat. *'What???'* he added, gazing back innocently at the suddenly shocked expressions turned towards him. 'I'm only saying.'

'Malcolm the Cat,' said King Toothbrush Weasel sternly, 'you are a very naughty army. You can't just go around killing people.'

'That's right,' agreed the wicked Witch of the East. 'Even if they do things like this.' And she turned King Toothbrush Weasel into a toad.

'Ribbit!' croaked King Toothbrush Weasel. 'What's happened?'

'Er . . . I'm afraid the wicked Witch has turned you into a toad, your majesty,' said Stinkbomb.

'But you're a very *sweet* little toad,' added Ketch-up-Face comfortingly.

'I don't *want* to be a sweet little toad!' King Toothbrush Weasel croaked. 'I want to go on being a king! Turn me back at once, horrible witch!'

'And what if I don't?' sneered the wicked Witch.

'Then,' *ribbited* King Toothbrush Weasel, 'I shall sting you painfully with my long venomous tentacles!'

'Toads don't have long venomous tentacles,' said Stinkbomb, 'I think you're thinking of jellyfish.'

'Oh,' said King Toothbrush Weasel. 'Really? What do toads do?'

'They go *ribbit*. And they crawl around.'

'Very well,' said King Toothbrush Weasel. 'Turn me back at once, horrible witch, or I shall go *ribbit* and crawl around!'

'Shan't,' said the wicked Witch of the East.

'Very well,' said King Toothbrush Weasel again. 'You asked for it.' And he went *ribbit* and crawled around. 'And you can stop looking at me like that, Malcolm the Cat,' he added. 'I'm the only one who knows where the royal tin-opener is.'

'Toto!' Dorothy gasped suddenly, for she had not seen her dog for several pages. 'Has anybody seen Toto?'

'And the Munchkins!' added the little woman. 'I'm sure there were supposed to be three Munchkins with me! We'd better go and look for them!'

And they hurried off.

'So what do we do now?' asked Ketchup-Face.

'We must try to find our way back to our own story,' said Miss Tibbles gravely, 'and hope that nothing else gets cut out or stuck in in the meantime.'

As the roar of the Doomsday Device faded to nothing, Draxxar threw back his head and laughed an **evil**, chilling laugh. The people of the planet Tharnos were dead. Now no one could stand in his way—except for Princess Zandara. Scowling as he thought of how she had escaped him, he opened the door to his spaceship.

There was a little girl inside. She was sitting at the controls of the spaceship making 'brrrm brrrm' noises.

'Hello,' she said, with a smile that showed the gap where she had recently lost a tooth.

'I'm Ketchup-Face, and this is my brother Stink-bomb.'

'Hello,' said Stinkbomb, who was getting into a spacesuit that was several sizes too big for him. 'You're Draxxar the Doombringer, destroyer of galaxies, aren't you?'

'Er, yes,' said Draxxar. 'What are you doing in my spaceship? There isn't supposed to be anyone on this planet but me. I've just killed everyone else.'

'That wasn't very kind,' said Ketchup-Face crossly.

'Don't worry,' said Stinkbomb, sitting down at the controls next to his sister. 'I've read this one. He gets defeated in the end, and gets sent to be a slave in the Mines of Jupiter.'

Ketchup-Face stuck out her tongue at Draxxar the Doombringer. 'Serves you right,' she said. 'You shouldn't go round killing people. It's naughty.'

'Yes, I suppose it is,' Draxxar admitted. 'I'd never really thought about it like that. But what are you doing in my spaceship? And who,' he added, 'are all these other people and animals and shopping trolleys? Get out at once, or I shall kill you all, even if it is naughty!' And he pointed his blaster at them to show that he meant it, and added, **'Ribbit! Ribbit!** What's happened?'

'Oh, dear,' said a kindly-looking librarianish woman. 'I'm afraid the wicked Witch of the East has turned you into a toad.'

'What???' Draxxar roared. 'But I don't want to be a toad! How am I going to conquer the universe if I'm a toad?'

'Don't care,' said a woman in a pointy hat, sticking out her tongue.

And then a cat in a red soldier's jacket pounced on Draxxar and pinned him to the floor.

But then it let him go.

But then it pounced on him again.

But then it let him go.

'Oh, do stop tormenting the poor creature, Malcolm the Cat,' said a toad with a crown and a badge saying 'King' and an expression which suggested it didn't really want to be a toad.

Sulkily, the cat let Draxxar the Doombringer go. Draxxar drew himself up to his full height, which wasn't very full now that he was a toad, and said, 'Well, even if I *am* a toad, I . . .

WAIT!!! DON'T TOUCH THAT LEVER!!!'

Stinkbomb paused, his hand a millimetre away from the lever, which was exactly the sort of lever that made you want to reach out and pull it. 'Why not?' he said.

'Because that's the hyperspace lever!' Draxxar croaked urgently. 'If you pull it without turning on the engines, every atom in our bodies will explode with the heat of a million fiery stars!'

Stinkbomb thought about this. The idea of every atom in his body exploding with the heat of a million fiery stars certainly sounded interesting, but on balance he wasn't sure if he fancied it. So he decided not to pull the lever.

'What does this button do?' asked Ketchup-Face interestedly, pressing a button.

The spaceship's engines burst into life.

'Oh,' said Stinkbomb. 'You've turned on the engines. I suppose that means I can pull the hyperspace lever now.'

And he pulled the hyperspace lever.

There was a judder, a shudder, a planet-shattering roar, and Draxxar the Doombringer's spaceship blasted off from Tharnos at impossible speed.

'Wheeeeeeeee!' shouted Ketchup-Face, and she burst into song:

'I'm flying into

At a very quick

With a smile upon my

It's a lovely

In fact it's completely

Maybe we'll find some aliens to

Or some meteors to

Though first I'll have to do up my shoe-

I wish I had a friend called

. . . Or Jemima or Harriet.

SPACE!!!!!!
PACE!!!!!!
FACE!!!!!!
PLACE!!!!!!!!!
ACE!!!!!!!!!!
CHASE!!!!!!!
RACE!!!!!!!!!
LACE!!!!!!
GRACE!!!!!

That's a song about flying into space,' she added.

'It's rubbish,' said the witch.

'No, it isn't,' said Ketchup-Face. 'It's a really really famous and excellent song that I've just made up. I expect witches don't know very much about songs.'

'Watch out for that meteor!' whimpered Draxxar.

Draxxar the Doombringer was not having a good day. It was true that he had ticked off the first item on his to-do list, which was 'kill everyone on Tharnos'. But on the other hand, Princess Zandara had escaped; he had been turned into a toad; his spaceship had been taken over by children and witches and librarians and cats and toads and shopping trolleys; and now he had a headache from being pounced on.

'Where are we going?' he asked.

'We're going to find Miss Butterworth,' said Ketchup-Face cheerily.

'And the library,' added Stinkbomb. 'What happens if I press this?'

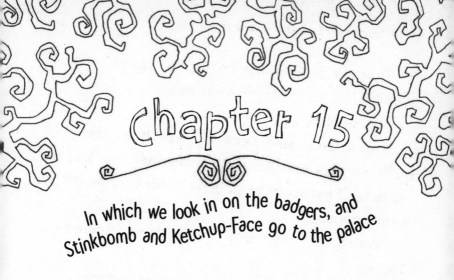

'That's funny,' muttered Harry the Badger.

Why's nothing happening in this **chapter**?'

Then he yelped.

'It's us! It's our bit! We're meant to be doing stuff!'

Immediately, all the other badgers leapt to their paws and tried to look busy.

'What are we meant to be doing?' asked Stewart the Badger, panicking slightly.

Harry the Badger looked at the **chapter heading**. 'Dunno,' he said. 'It just says the readers are looking in on us.'

'Oooh,'

said all the other badgers.

'Hello, readers!'

They all began waving, even though there wasn't a picture of this bit so nobody could see them.

'Hang on,' Harry the Badger added. 'It says Stinkbomb and Ketchup-Face are in this **chapter**, too!' He skipped down to the next section, moving his lips as he read.

'Oh no! Quick, Stewart the Badger! Pass me a bit of another story!'

'What sort of story?' asked Stewart the Badger.

'It doesn't matter!!!' said Harry the Badger.

'Just pass me some more pages, quick!!! They're in the next paragraph!!!!!'

ⓔ　ⓔ　ⓔ

'How did we get here?' asked Stinkbomb.

'I suppose we must have reached the end of the bits the badgers have stuck in,' said Miss Tibbles. 'We'd better hurry, before they stick

108

The Owl and the Pussy-Cat

The Owl and the Pussy-Cat went to sea
In a beautiful pea-green boat.
They took some honey, and plenty of money
Wrapped up in a five-pound note.
The Owl looked up to the stars above,
And sang to a small guitar,
'O lovely Pussy! O Pussy, my love,
What a beautiful Pussy you are,
You are,
You are!
What a beautiful Pussy you are!'

Pussy said to the Owl, 'You elegant fowl!
How charmingly sweet you sing!
But who are these children? And what are these toads?
Why is one of them dressed as a king?'

The Owl beheld a librarian, too,
And a witch; and he thought it was folly
To be taking a witch in the back of a boat
With a sweet little squeaky-wheeled trolley
Wheeled trolley
Wheeled trolley
With a sweet little squeaky-wheeled trolley.

Said the Owl to the Cat, 'I do not recall that
Being part of the plan. Did you pack it?'
But the Pussy said naught. Her attention was caught
By a cat in a red soldier's jacket.

Alfred Kendon-Furtado put his hand up. 'Excuse me,' he said. 'I'm supposed to be in the story, you know. So if you're all suddenly in a poem, why aren't I in the poem as well?'

'I'm afraid it's because,' the librarian said,
  After scratching her head for a minute,
'You don't get to be properly part of a tale
  Just by winning the chance to be in it
    Be in it
    Be in it
  Just by winning the chance to be in it.'

'Dear Pussy, I think we are likely to sink,'
  Said the Owl, 'with these folk in our boat.
Significant dangers are posed by these strangers.
  They're too heavy to keep us afloat.

Let us ask them to leave, and continue in peace,'
But the Pussy said nothing to that.
She just gave him a shove; for she'd fallen in love
With that elegant Malcolm the Cat
The Cat
The Cat
With that elegant Malcolm the Cat.

zombie teachers shuffling towards them.

'Zombies!' said Stinkbomb. 'Great! I've always wanted to be in a story with zombies!'

'Zombie teachers!' said Ketchup-Face happily. 'I've read this story. It's really good.'

'That's nice,' said Miss Tibbles, 'but . . . well . . .

ZOMBIES!!!!!!! THEY'LL TEAR US APART AND EAT OUR BRAINS!!!'

Stinkbomb thought about this. The idea of zombies tearing him apart and eating his brains certainly sounded interesting, but on balance he wasn't sure if he fancied it. 'Fair point,' he said.

'RUN!!!!!'

So they ran—except for the Owl, who flew, and King Toothbrush Weasel and Draxxar the Doombringer, who crawled and went **'ribbit'**, and the little shopping trolley, who trundled.

'UUUURGH!'

the zombie teachers moaned.

'MAAAAAAATHS! MAAAAAAATHS!'

They hurtled down the long, dimly lit corridor in which they found themselves. The lights flickered eerily as they ran; shadows leapt out at

them. And from behind them came the horrible scraping sound of zombie teachers shuffling ever forwards.

'It's a bit spooky, isn't it,' said Ketchup-Face cheerily.

And then, suddenly, in front of them stood a blank grey wall. They could hear the zombie teachers **shuffling closer, closer, closer, groaning,**

'MAAAAAAATHS! MAAAAAAATHS!!!'

They were trapped.

Alfred Kendon-Furtado put his hand up.

'Excuse me,' he said. 'My mum let me enter this competition because she thought it would be fun. She'll be very cross if I get eaten by zombies.'

'What do we do?' asked Miss Tibbles.

'If I were not a toad, I could blast those zombies into dust!' said Draxxar the Doombringer.

'Yes,' said Stinkbomb, 'but you are a toad.'

'Maybe the wicked Witch could turn the zombies into toads,' suggested Miss Tibbles hopefully.

The wicked Witch stuck her tongue out rudely. 'Shan't,' she said. 'I like zombies.'

'Perhaps the army should do something,' suggested King Toothbrush Weasel. **'Ribbit.'**

'Don't you dare put Malcolm the Cat in danger!' the Pussy-Cat said. 'I love him!'

The zombie teachers stopped shuffling forwards.

'OOOOOOOOOOO-OOOOOOOOOOOH!'

they said, making kissing sounds. Then they went back to shuffling forwards. **'MAAAATHS!**

MAAAAATHS!!!' they moaned, **getting closer** and **closer** and **closer**, their horrible hands reaching out.

'Does anyone know how to stop zombie teachers?' said Stinkbomb, looking pointedly at Ketchup-Face. 'Maybe . . . someone who's read the book?'

Ketchup-Face cleared her throat importantly. 'I've read the book,' she said proudly. 'I know all about zombie teachers. And I can tell you . . . ' She paused for dramatic effect.

'Yes???' said everyone else, less for dramatic effect than because a load of flesh-eating zombie teachers were only metres away from tearing them apart and eating their brains.

'I can tell you,' Ketchup-Face repeated with the confidence of an expert, 'that there is absolutely no way to stop zombie teachers.'

'Oh,' said everyone else, more than a little disappointed.

'However,' Ketchup-Face went on, 'this is not an ordinary wall. It's the secret entrance to the secret laboratory of the **evil** Doctor Arno Schrodinger, creator of the zombie teachers!

Ta-daaaaah!'

She pressed a secret button. The wall slid open, revealing a gleaming but sinister laboratory.

'Inside! Quick!' yelled Stinkbomb—rather unnecessarily, since everybody had rushed forward the moment the wall had opened. It closed behind them, shutting the zombie teachers out.

'Phew!' said Miss Tibbles. 'Safe!'

'Er . . . I don't think we are, actually,' said the little shopping trolley. 'Look!'

There was a tall, thin, cruel-looking man in the laboratory.

'It's Doctor Arno Schrodinger!' said Ketchup-Face. 'He's the bad guy.'

'Oh, look!' said Doctor Schrodinger. 'Just what I need for my latest **evil** scientific experiment—a cat!' He grabbed Malcolm the Cat and—ignoring the protests of the Pussy-Cat—put him in a box. 'This,' he said,

'is my
Evil Box
of Death.'

He pressed a button on the box. 'If it works, then the inside of the box is now full of **evil deathness** and a **dead cat.**' He paused, thinking. 'But if it has worked, then if I open the box all the **evil deathness** will get out and **deathify** everybody.' He scratched his head. 'I'm not sure what to do now. Opening the box is the only way of telling if the cat is dead.'

'No, it isn't,' said Stinkbomb, and he knocked on the box and said, 'Hey! Malcolm the Cat! Are you dead?'

Yes, I am.

There was a pause, and then Malcolm the Cat's voice came from inside the box.

'Yes,' it said. 'Yes, I am.'

The Pussy-Cat began to yowl in anguish.

'Though, actually,' Malcolm the Cat continued, 'perhaps I'm not dead after all.'

The Pussy-Cat stopped yowling in anguish.

'Or maybe I am,' said Malcolm the Cat.

The Pussy-Cat wailed piteously.

'Or perhaps I'm not,' said Malcolm the Cat.

The Pussy-Cat stopped wailing piteously.

'Or . . . wait . . . no, sorry,' said Malcolm the Cat. 'My mistake. I'm definitely dead.'

The Pussy-Cat wept bitterly.

'On the other hand . . .' said Malcolm the Cat.

'Oh, this is ridiculous,' said Doctor Schrodinger in disgust. 'We still don't know if he's dead. I'll have to go and invent a **Looking-At-Cats-In-Boxes device.'**

He went to a door at the other end of the laboratory, and opened it. A zombie teacher came in.

'Oh, hello,' said Doctor Schrodinger. 'Since you're here, would you mind guarding these people for a few minutes?' And he left the room.

The zombie teacher lurched menacingly forwards. **'MAAAATHS!'** it said **'MAAAAATHS!!!'**

'Oh, dear,' said Miss Tibbles nervously. 'Miss Butterworth would be really useful right now. I hope we get back to our own story and find the library soon.'

'This is fun!' said Rolf the Badger enthusiastically. 'What shall we do next?'

Harry the Badger held up the by now very battered copy of Stinkbomb & Ketchup-Face and the Great Big Story Nickers. 'With this book, Rolf the Badger,' he said, 'we can do anything we want! We can get Stinkbomb and Ketchup-Face trapped by zombies, or witches, or **evil** galactic doombringers, or um, owls and pussy-cats! And if we want something nice to happen to us, we just have to write it into the story!'

'Write "And then she did a poo,"' sniggered one of the other badgers, who still wasn't keeping up.

'And the best bit,' Harry the Badger went on, 'is that Stinkbomb and Ketchup-Face will never stop us! They won't even be able to find us!'

'We've found them!' yelled Stinkbomb.

'Stop them!' shouted Ketchup-Face.

'Yay!' said Alfred Kendon-Furtado.

'It's the badgers!'

'Where did they come from?' said Harry the Badger. 'Quick! Write something in the book!'

'Where's the pen?' yelped Rolf the Badger. 'Where's the pen?'

'Maaaaaths!' moaned the zombie teacher.

'**Ribbit!**' said King Toothbrush Weasel and Draxxar the Doombringer.

'Where's the pen?!?' yelped Rolf the Badger again.

'What are they doing back here?' demanded Harry the Badger. 'Why didn't you rip the next **chapter** out?'

'Er, because we were in it,' said Stewart the Badger. 'I mean, we are in it. Now.'

'Well, rip it out anyway!' Harry the Badger ordered.

'No!' said Miss Tibbles. 'If you rip out the **chapter** that we're in, just as it's happening, it might mean **doom** for us all!'

'Yay! I like **dooms!**' said Stewart the Badger, who thought that a **doom** was a kind of bouncy castle, and he reached for the page to rip it out.

127

'NO!'

yelled Harry the Badger, who wasn't quite sure what a **doom** was but was sure it was much less fun than a bouncy castle; and he grabbed the book from Stewart the Badger, and ran.

Then there was chaos, as Stinkbomb and Ketchup-Face chased Harry the Badger. All the other badgers chased Stinkbomb and Ketchup-Face. Miss Tibbles and the little shopping trolley chased all the other badgers. The zombie teacher got in the way. The wicked Witch of the East tripped people up and laughed rudely.

No!

King Toothbrush Weasel and Draxxar the Doom-bringer went **'ribbit'** and crawled around. Malcolm the Cat joined in the chase. And then he didn't. And then he did. And then he didn't. The Pussy-Cat chased Malcolm the Cat, except when he wasn't joining in the chase. The Owl sulked in the corner because nothing rhymed and the Pussy-Cat had fallen in love with Malcolm the Cat. Alfred Kendon-Furtado kept trying to stop the badgers and get their autographs. And some comedy saxophone music played in the background, because it was that sort of chase scene.

It could have gone on for a long time; but Harry the Badger grabbed the nearest book from the floor and—without even looking to see what it was—tore out some pages and stuck them in.

XI
What I Heard
in the Apple Barrel

'No, not I,' said Silver. 'Flint was cap'n; I was quartermaster, along of my timber leg . . . '

'Ooh, I've read this book! It's Treasure Island!' said another voice. 'This is the bit where Jim Hawkins hides in a big barrel and finds out that Long John Silver and most of the other sailors are really pirates!'

The apple barrel was not so empty as I had believed. It was difficult to be certain in the darkness, but it seemed to contain at least two children, quite as many cats and toads, and a wheeled basket made of shining metal. In addition, something that felt like the tip of a pointy hat was digging hard into my back; something large and heavy pressed against my nose, filling my nostrils with the stench of death; and there was a librarian sitting on my head.

'Ewwww,' said another voice, even younger than the first. 'What's that stinky smell? Has somebody farted?'

'I think that might be the zombie teacher,' said the first voice.

'Maaaaths!'

intoned a third.

'Hello!' said the first speaker, his voice now right by my ear. Turning my head with difficulty, I perceived that he was a boy. 'I'm Stinkbomb,' he said to me. 'You must be Jim Hawkins. This is a great story! You're doing a really good job of narrating it.'

'Here!' Silver said sharply. 'Who's that a-speaking from the apple barrel?'

'Arrr!' said one of the deckhands. 'And what be all them badgers a-doin', stickin' out the top like that?'

Next second, the apple barrel was heaved onto its side, and out I tumbled; but Silver scarce seemed to notice me, next to the strange assortment of creatures that had spilled out on to the deck.

'So!' Silver roared. 'Stowaways and spies, I'll be bound!'

'No,' said a little girl with a gap-toothed smile. 'Stinkbomb and Ketchup-Face. We're trying to find the library and rescue Miss Butterworth.'

'Toads and badgers everywhere!' said Israel Hands, the coxswain. ''Tis witchery!'

'What's wrong with that?' said the woman in the pointy hat indignantly, and she turned Israel Hands into a toad.

'RIBBIT!' said Israel Hands. 'What's a-going on?'

'Witchcraft!' cried Silver. 'But we knows

how to deal with a witch, don't we, me hearties!'

'That we do!' agreed the deckhands, and as one man they took hold of the witch and threw her over the side of the ship. She disappeared for a moment beneath the brine and then rose sharply to the surface, the water bubbling EVILLY around her.

'I'm melting!' she cried. 'I'm melting! Didn't you know that water would be the death of me?!'

'Oooh,' said the little girl—who I took to be Ketchup-Face. 'The sea's gone all fizzy!'

'RIBBIT!' said Israel Hands again.

Within moments, there was nothing left of the witch but a pointy hat and a pair of silver shoes, which bobbed away on the waves and disappeared from view.

'Oh, dear,' said the wheeled basket.

'Yes,' said the librarian. 'It does seem a bit harsh, doesn't it? But after all, she was supposed to have been squashed by a house several chapters ago.'

'Now,' said Silver. 'What about you badgers, eh! You'll be after our treasure, I'll be bound! Shall we make 'em walk the plank, lads?'

'Arrrrr!'

roared the crewmen—who I now understood to be pirates—and they seized hold of the badgers.

'Are we going to our doom?' said the smallest of the badgers, in what sounded oddly like a tone of excitement.

'Don't you worry, Stewart the Badger,' said another badger, taking a sip of tea from a mug marked World's Best Badger. 'Leave it to me. I'll handle this.

Now, then, Mr Pirate,' he said, looking up at Long John Silver.

'You don't want to be making us walk the plank.'

Silver thought about this for a moment.

'Yes, we do,'

he said.

'Oh,' said the badger. 'Um . . . Are you sure?'

'That I am,' said Silver. 'Up you hop.'

Next second, several of the pirates had produced knives and cutlasses, and were prodding the badgers onto a very long plank.

'I don't like this,' said a big badger with a big badge that said, (Big Badger). 'What are we going to do, Harry the Badger?'

Harry the Badger, the one who had spoken to Silver, held up a strange and brightly-coloured book. 'Who's got the pen?' he asked, edging along the plank away from the pirates' blades.

'Here it is,' said Stewart the Badger cheerfully, passing it back along the line of badgers

towards him. 'Whoops,' he added, dropping it into the waves below. The badgers leaned over mournfully and watched it fall.

'Bother!' said Harry the Badger. 'That's just typical. And stop poking me with that pointy thing!' he added, snapping in irritation at one of the deckhands.

'Sorry,' said the deckhand. Then he said, 'Wait a minute! I'm a pirate! I'm not sorry at all!' and began to poke the badgers once more.

They edged away, until the plank bent under the weight of an enormous pile of badgers. The crewmen cheered and jeered and begged Long John Silver to be allowed to push them into the icy sea below.

'As if today wasn't going badly enough,' complained Harry the Badger, 'I've just trod in something sticky.'

'Ewwwww,' said the other badgers.

'I expect that'll be ship's tar,' said Stink-bomb knowledgeably. 'They used a lot of tar on sailing ships.'

'Is that so?' said Harry the Badger, a cunning gleam coming into his eye. He reached down and scraped the blob of tar onto one claw. Then he opened the book, and with that claw wrote something in tar upon its pages.

And then the badgers went back to the librarry.

'How did they do that?' said Silver.

Another boy—whom I had not before noticed—put his hand up. 'Excuse me!' he said. 'This is completely the wrong story! I'm not supposed to be in this one!'

'Oooh!' said all the pirates. 'Are we in a story?' And they began to comb their beards and straighten their neckerchiefs.

'That's really not the point,' said the boy. 'The point is that I won a competition to be in the new Stinkbomb and Ketchup-Face story, not *Treasure Island.'*

'Hang on!' said Stinkbomb excitedly. 'Look! While Alfred was speaking, we seem to have arrived back in Great Kerfuffle! We're in the library!'

'Look!' said Ketchup-Face excitedly. 'There's Miss Butterworth! We've found her! Oh—and there's . . . er . . . me. And you, Stinkbomb. And Malcolm the Cat. And King Toothbrush Weasel, except he isn't a toad!'

'Oh,' said King Toothbrush Weasel. 'How did I stop being a toad? **Ribbit!'**

'Er, no,' said Stinkbomb. 'You're still a toad. It's the other King Toothbrush Weasel who isn't a toad—the one who's over there, next to the other Stinkbomb and the other Ketchup-Face and the other Malcolm the Cat.'

`'Oooh,'

said one of the pirates excitedly.

`'Look at all these books! Can we have a story?'`

'Of course!' said Miss Tibbles. 'I'm sure I can find a lovely story which will be just right for a lot of **pirates** and a **cabin boy** and a **zombie teacher** and an **owl** and a **pussy-cat** and some **toads** who used to be **kings** and **pirates** and **destroyers of galaxies**. Oh, look! Here's one called *The Pirates and the Cabin Boy and the Zombie Teacher and the Owl and the Pussy-Cat and the Toads who used to be Kings and Pirates and Destroyers of Galaxies Have a Lovely Day Out at the Seaside!*'

'Hooray!'

said the pirates and the cabin boy and the owl and the pussy-cat and the toads who used to be kings and pirates and destroyers of galaxies, and they all settled down to listen.

'Maaaaaths!'

said the zombie teacher, and he settled down to listen too.

'Thank goodness for that,' said Stinkbomb, as they made their way over to Miss Butterworth. 'It had got to the point where there were just too many characters in this story.'

'Miss Butterworth!' yelled Ketchup-Face happily, pushing past a very startled Ketchup-Face and flinging herself into the ninja librarian's arms.

Miss Butterworth looked from one Ketchup-Face to the other. *'O, jeetje,'* she said.

'What?' said Ketchup-Face.

'Watte?' said the other Ketchup-Face.

'What are you talking like that for?' asked Stinkbomb.

'Waarom praat je zo raar?' asked the other Stinkbomb.

'This is a bit strange,' said Malcolm the Cat.

'Or . . . perhaps it isn't.

But then again, perhaps it is.

Although . . .'

'Au!' said the other Malcolm the Cat.

'O, sorry,' said Miss Butterworth, looking down and taking her foot off the other Malcolm the Cat's tail.

Au!

'I don't understand!'

said Ketchup-Face exasperatedly. 'If we're back in our own book, why is everybody speaking so strangely?'

'It sounds like double-Dutch to me,' agreed Stinkbomb.

'Er . . . it sounds like single Dutch to me,' said the little shopping trolley shyly. 'I mean, I think they're speaking Dutch.'

'But why would they be speaking Dutch, the sillies?' asked Ketchup-Face.

'Well,' said the little shopping trolley, 'you know how the badgers have been sticking bits of other books into this one? Maybe this page is from the Dutch version of one of your books.'

Miss Butterworth turned to a bookshelf and took down a book entitled *Engels voor Ninja-Bibliothecaressen*, which is Dutch for *English for Ninja Librarians*. She read it quickly, and then looked up and said, *'Greetings, English translations of Stinkbom en Ketchupkop. I am juffrouw Van Dalen.'*

`'Hello, Yuffrow Vandaling . . . er . . . Yuffer Violin . . . er . . . Shuffly Mandolin . . .'`

Ketchup-Face said.

The ninja librarian looked down kindly at her.

'You may call me Dutch Miss Butterworth,' she said. *'What are you doing here?'*

Stinkbomb and Ketchup-Face explained.

'Ah,' said Dutch Miss Butterworth. 'I see. Hmmm. We must get you back to your own story immediately. Come with me, Stinkbomb and Ketchup-Face. Just you two,' she added. 'This will not work with more than two characters, which is actually quite lucky, since there are still far too many characters in this story.'

Alfred Kendon-Furtado put his hand up. 'Excuse me,' he said. 'What about me?'

'Who are you?' asked Dutch Miss Butterworth.

'I'm Alfred Kendon-Furtado,' said Alfred Kendon-Furtado. 'I won the competition. To be in the story.'

'Ah,' said Dutch Miss Butterworth wisely. 'I am afraid that since you are not a proper character, this will not work for you. But I suspect that, if you have won a competition to be in the story, you will find yourself in it regardless. Now—Stinkbomb and Ketchup-Face, come with me.'

Stinkbomb and Ketchup-Face went with her.

Dutch Miss Butterworth opened a door. 'This,' she said, 'is one of the many secret doors which may be found in every true library. Go through it, and you will find yourself back in the story in which you belong.'

'Gosh,' said Stinkbomb. 'That's handy.'

'It is indeed,' said Dutch Miss Butterworth. 'As a matter of fact, I don't think it has ever been used before. Now: go through the door.'

Stinkbomb and Ketchup-Face went through the door.

chapter 23

In which Stinkbomb & Ketchup-Face finally find themselves back in Stinkbomb & Ketchup-Face and the Great Big Story Nickers

On the other side of the door, they found themselves in the library.

It was full of ninja librarians.

'That's odd,' said Stinkbomb. 'I thought Miss Butterworth was the only ninja librarian in Great Kerfuffle.'

'Er . . . yeah,' said one of the ninja librarians. 'Normally. But . . . er . . . she had to go away. And, er, she asked us to help till she got back.

151

Isn't that right, ninja librarians?'

'Oh, yes,' agreed all the other ninja librarians.

'Well,' said Ketchup-Face, 'since Miss Butter-worth isn't here, maybe you can help us put the story right again.'

'Er . . . ' said the first ninja librarian uncertainly, 'I think we're a bit busy. We've got books to take off the shelves, and books to put back on the shelves, and books to knock over, and books to frighten, and books to drive too fast.'

'Oh,' said Ketchup-Face. 'Um . . . OK.'

Stinkbomb was unaccountably suspicious. 'Are you *sure* you're ninja librarians?'

'Oh, yes,' said the ninja librarian. 'We're definitely ninja librarians. We're very ninja librariany indeed. Isn't that right, Rolf the Ninja Librarian?'

'That's right,' agreed Rolf the Ninja Librarian, a big ninja librarian with a big badge that said

. 'We're ninja librarians all right. Aren't we, Harry the Ninja Librarian?'

'Yes,' agreed Harry the Ninja Librarian, taking a sip of tea from a mug marked, . 'We're extremely ninja librariany. Aren't we, Stewart the Ninja Librarian?'

Just as Stewart the Ninja Librarian was opening his mouth to answer, Harry the Ninja Librarian passed him a note that said:

Pretend we're ninja librarians.

Stewart the Ninja Librarian read it slowly three times and then said, 'Er, we're ninja librarians.' He turned the note over. On the other side it said:

Don't let them know we're badgers.

'Er, we're not badgers,' he added.

'Well, if you're sure,' Stinkbomb said. 'Ooh,' he added, noticing that Stewart the Ninja Librarian was holding a book, 'is that a book about us?'

Stewart the Ninja Librarian looked guiltily at the book. It was called Stinkbomb & Ketchup-Face and the Great Big Story Nickers, although somebody had written a **K** by the word **Nickers**. 'Er . . . no,' he said.

'It looks like a book about us,' said Ketchup-Face. 'It's got our names on it and everything.'

'Can I have a look?' asked Stinkbomb, reaching for it.

Stewart the Ninja Librarian looked uncertainly at Harry the Ninja Librarian.

'No!' said Harry the Ninja Librarian sharply,

snatching the book out of Stewart the Ninja Librarian's paws.

'Hang on,' said Stinkbomb. 'I didn't know ninja librarians had paws!'

'Miss Butterworth doesn't have paws,' Ketchup-Face added.

'Ah,' said Harry the Ninja Librarian shiftily. 'Er . . . yes. The paws. Um . . . we've got paws because . . . er . . . Why have we got paws, Rolf the Ninja Librarian?'

'Er . . . Dunno,' said Rolf the Ninja Librarian. 'Why've we got paws, Stewart the Ninja Librarian?'

'Um . . . ' said Stewart the Ninja Librarian, 'is it because we're badgers?'

'Yes,' said Harry the Ninja Librarian. 'I expect that's it.'

Ketchup-Face gasped **gymnastically**, forgetting she'd already decided that drama was best for gasping. 'You're the badgers!' she said, pointing.

'Bother,' said Harry the Ninja Librarian, who was really Harry the Badger. 'Rumbled.'

'It's rude to point,' said Rolf the Ninja Librarian, who was really Rolf the Badger.

'It's even ruder to break out of prison and spoil a story and pretend to be ninja librarians,' Ketchup-Face said.

'Yeah, fair point,' said Rolf the Badger. 'I forgot.'

'Anyway,' said Stinkbomb, reaching for the book, 'now we're going to thwart you.'

'No you aren't!' said Harry the Badger **evilly** and **wickedly**; and holding the book out of Stinkbomb's reach, he turned hurriedly to **page 158**.

'Stop, you naughty!' said Ketchup-Face.

Harry the Badger ignored her. Taking out a pen, he found a blank space at the end of **Chapter Twenty-Three**, and wrote something.

And suddinly stinkbomb and ketchup-face needed a wee really really badly.

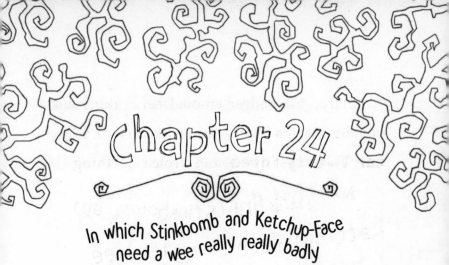

chapter 24

In which Stinkbomb and Ketchup-Face
need a wee really really badly

'Stinkbomb!' gasped Ketchup-Face, wriggling and squirming like a squiggly worm.

'I need a wee really really badly!'

'Me too,' said Stinkbomb, going a bit pink with the effort of holding it in. 'But we can't stop in the middle of thwarting the badgers just to go to the loo!'

And with all the strength of will he possessed,

he ignored the really bad needing-a-wee feeling, and advanced on Harry the Badger.

But Harry the Badger found the next blank bit of page and wrote some more.

Now Stinkbomb needed the loo so badly a little bit of wee came out and went in his pants.

chapter 25

In which Stinkbomb has to run to the loo

Stinkbomb went bright red. 'I . . . er . . . I don't think I can hold it in any more!' he gasped, and ran to the loo.

'That was horrid!' said Ketchup-Face, crossing her legs and advancing on Harry the Badger.

Harry the Badger just laughed an **evil** and **wicked** laugh, and poked Ketchup-Face in the tummy. Ketchup-Face made a funny little squeaky noise and dashed after Stinkbomb.

Harry the Badger climbed on a table.

'Badgers!'

he said.

'After almost five books, we have at last won!'

'Yay!'

cheered all the badgers, and they did a dance all the way round the library.

'It feels a bit funny, doesn't it,' said Rolf the Badger. 'I'm not used to us winning.'

'What about Miss Butterworth?' asked Stewart the Badger. 'Is she going to thwart us?'

162

'Nope,' said Harry the Badger smugly. 'I locked her in a cupboard.'

'So . . . er . . . what happens now?' asked Rolf the Badger.

'Now?' said Harry the Badger, waving *Stinkbomb & Ketchup-Face and the Great Big Story Nickers*. 'Now we can do anything! We can write ourselves worms to eat and dustbins to knock over and cars to drive too fast, and we can write me being king, and we can write us having all the money in the world, and we can write us chickens to frighten and lawns to dig up and anything we want! And nobody can stop us! Specially not you two,' he added, sticking his tongue out at Stinkbomb and Ketchup-Face, who were just coming back from the toilet. 'Stop right there!' He turned to **page 164**.

'Or I'll make you really really need a poo, and I'll write the toilet door locked!'

Stinkbomb and Ketchup-Face stopped, and looked at each other. 'What do we do now?' asked Ketchup-Face quietly.

'I'm not sure,' said Stinkbomb. 'The whole thing seems to have got completely out of hand.'

'Well,' said Ketchup-Face, 'at least we ought to say something brave and heroic.' And raising her voice, she called defiantly: 'You'll never get away with this!'

'Oh, yeah?' said Harry the Badger, raising the book high. 'Who says?!?'

'*I* say!' said Alfred Kendon-Furtado, snatching the book from Harry the Badger's paw.

The badgers gasped geographically, for they really hadn't got the hang of the whole gasping thing at all.

'Who are you?' demanded Harry the Badger.

Alfred Kendon-Furtado took a deep breath. 'I'm Alfred Kendon-Furtado,' he said. 'I won the competition. To be in the story. *This* story. And you badgers have spoiled it. Well, I'm going to do *something* useful before it's over! But, um, just before I do . . . Could we have a selfie?'

'OK,' said Harry the Badger, and the entire story stopped while the badgers all gathered round Alfred, who took several pictures of himself with the badgers and finally managed to do one that got everyone in.

'Thanks,' said Alfred. 'Now, where was I?

Oh, yes—I'm going to do something useful before the whole story is over!'

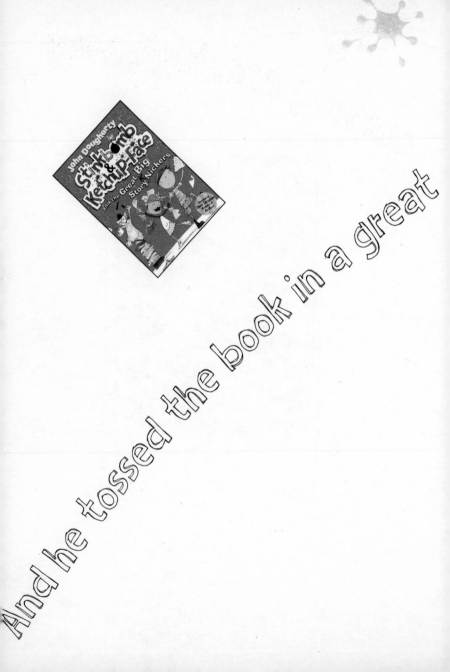

And he tossed the book in a great

curving arc, high over

the badgers' heads and

right into Stinkbomb's hand.

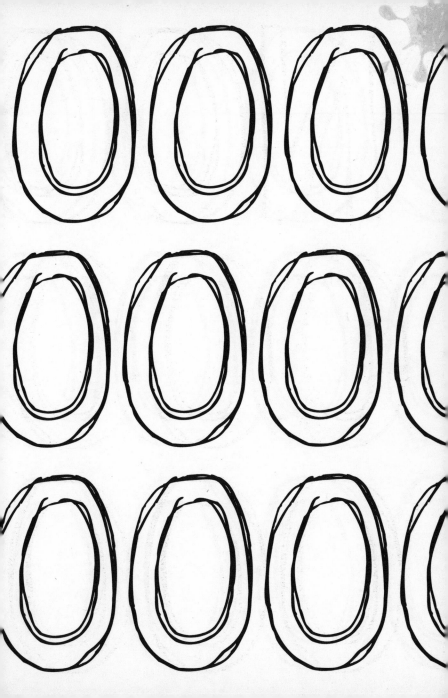

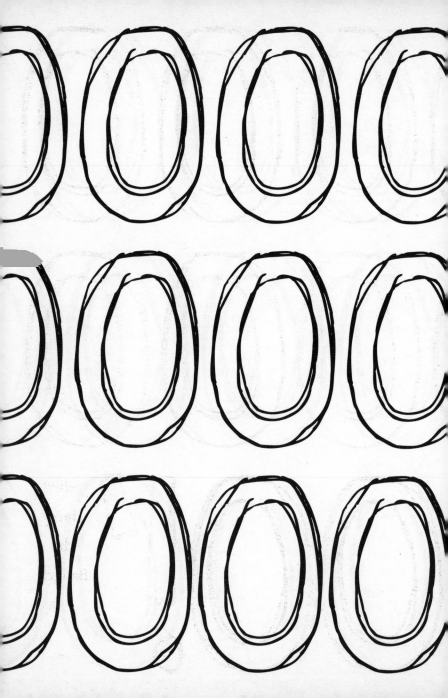

OOOOOO OOOOOO OO!

yelled
Harry
the
Badger.

And before the badgers could stop them, Stink-bomb and Ketchup-Face had found the **chapter** they were in and written their own bits at the end.

Then Stinkbomb did some amazing martial arts moves and frightened all the badgers so much that they ran back to jail and locked themselves in.

And Ketchup-Face resquooed Miss Butterworth and had sum cake.

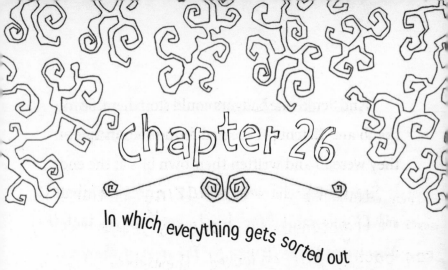

chapter 26

In which everything gets sorted out

It took Stinkbomb and Ketchup-Face quite some time to explain everything to Miss Butterworth.

'So,' the ninja librarian said when they had finished, '*there is much to repair. King Tooth-brush Weasel is still a toad, and we must find a way to bring him and the little shopping trolley and Malcolm the Cat and Miss Tibbles back to Great Kerfuffle before the end of this story.*'

'And,' said Ketchup-Face, 'we haven't started the Great Kerfuffle Great Summer Read yet.'

'Oh, look,' said Stinkbomb. 'What's that on the floor? It looks like a **chapter** from one of our books!'

Miss Butterworth picked it up. *'Chapter eight,'* she said. *'The very chapter where everybody comes to the library for the start of the Great Kerfuffle Great Summer Read. I wonder . . . '* She paused, thoughtfully, and a look of determination came over her face. *'Children,'* she said, picking up the mutilated copy of Stink-bomb & Ketchup-Face **and the Great Big Story Nickers**, *'pass me the sticky tape.'*

chapter 8

The library was absolutely buzzing. Everybody in Loose Chippings was there for the official opening of the Great Kerfuffle Great Summer Read.

'Well, that seemed to work!' said Stinkbomb.

'I now declare the Great Kerfuffle Great Summer Read officially open!' said King Toothbrush Weasel, to tremendous applause; and added, '**Ribbit!** Oh, dear; I appear to still be a weevil . . . '

'Toad, your majesty,' Stinkbomb said.

'Oh. Oh, yes,' said King Toothbrush Weasel. 'I appear to still be a toad, with long venomous tentacles and . . .'

'No, you silly king,' said Ketchup-Face. 'Just the **ribbitty** crawly kind of toad.'

'Yes, well,' said King Toothbrush Weasel. 'The point is, I'm not the personny kind of king. Does anyone know how to fix me?'

'I think you need a kiss from a real princess,' said Ketchup-Face.

'Real princesses are all very well,' said Miss Butterworth, *'but for the true magic of a story, you need a real librarian.'*

'Ewwww,' said Miss Tibbles. 'I'm not sure I want to kiss a toad.'

'Heads or tails?' said Miss Butterworth.

Miss Butterworth won, and Miss Tibbles had to kiss King Toothbrush Weasel, who immediately turned back into a real king again and began **kinging** for all he was worth.

So all was well again upon the little island of Great Kerfuffle. In the trees, the birds **twittered** and **tweeted**. In the ponds, the newts swam; and the frogs **croaked**; and the toads **sang** about fifteen toads on a dead toad's chest, and plotted the destruction of galaxies. In the harbour, an owl was trying to persuade a pussy-cat to forget about the army and go to sea in a beautiful pea-green boat. Through the woodland a zombie teacher roamed, moaning `Maaaaaths!' happily to itself and terrifying the woodland creatures. In the jail, the badgers plotted **evil** and **wicked** plots.

And in the library, all the residents of Loose Chippings were choosing their books for the Great Summer Read. Miss Butterworth and Miss Tibbles were chatting to Alfred Kendon-Furtado, who had well and truly become part of the story just in time. And Stinkbomb and Ketchup-Face thought that only one thing could make their happiness complete. Then, through the tall book-stacks, they glimpsed two familiar figures making their way towards them.

'HELLO, MY DARLINGS!'

came their mother's voice from behind the bookshelves. 'Can we come out? Has the story finished yet?'

'Yes,' said Ketchup-Face happily.

like to

make up

story?'

Write a Story the Ketchup-Face Way!

by Ketchup-Face

Every story needs three things:

1 a beginning
2 a middle
3 a horsey

though I expect you can get away without the middle if you really want.

A good beginning for a story is:

Wunce uppon a time, there wos a byooteyfull horsey called Starlite.

Most stories really ought to begin this way. The one thing you DON'T want at the beginning of your story is a blackbird. 'Cos blackbirds are rubbish. And a bit loud. Especially when you're trying to sleep.

Anyway, once you have a beginning, you need a problem.

The buteyfool horsey had a problem. He thougt he was a shoping trolly. This was a problum beckuz he was a horsey.

The problam was even worse beckuz he wos not a shopping trolly. He wos a byutiffle horsey. But evrywer he went, he sed no i am not a biooooooteefuol horsey. i am a litl shoping trolly.

Then you need to make the problem even worse.

But wun day allong came a litl girl. She wos a verry clevver litl girl as wel as being verry talinted and a good singer. She sang him a song.

Then you need a way of solving the problem. Most problems can be solved with cake.

Oh wat a luvly song sed the horsey.

Yes, sed the litl girl. Hav sum cake.

Then the beotiful horsy had sum cake, and then it sed o i remember now. I am a horsey not a shoping trolly.

Silly me. Wood you like to go for a galup.

Yes pleez sed the litl girl.

And they all livd hapilee evver after. The end.

Acknowledgements

A very big 'dank je' (did I get that right?) to the fabulous Sandra Hessels for help with all the Dutch bits, and to Bert and all at Stinkbomb & Ketchup-Face's Dutch publisher, Veltman Uitgevers, for your help in making that happen.

Thank you to everyone who entered the competition to be in the book, and particularly to Alfred Kendon-Furtado for winning it.

Thanks too to Rudyard Kipling, Lewis Carroll, L Frank Baum, Edward Lear, and Robert Louis Stevenson for writing some of the books that the badgers vandalised, and for dying more than seventy years ago so that I could use some of their words in this book.

Big thanks to my editor, Kathy Webb, and our designer, Karen Stewart, for all the extra work they had to do after the badgers got hold of the book and started messing around with it.

And of course, thank you always to Noah and Cara, not only for being my chief inspirations for Stinkbomb and Ketchup-Face but also for all your help, suggestions, and encouragement. You guys are the best.

Photo © Michael Dannenberg

John Dougherty

(Author)

This season I'd rather be writing about ~~foxes~~ badgers.

Illustration by Stanley Tazzyman

David Tazzyman

(Illustrator)

This season I'd rather be drawing ~~foxes~~ badgers.

Ready for more great stories?
Try one of these . . .

coming soon

Ooh look . . . more funny books, and one of them even has badgers in it!